For little Emily to read
when she's older.

Special thanks to Andy
for his constant support.

Collect books by Helen Wendy Cooper

SHAPE LAND – Trevor Triangle Loses the Mail

SHAPE LAND – Silly Samuel Square

www.helenwendycooper.co.uk

Contents

– Helen Wendy Cooper –

The Vegetarian Vampire: Halloween Disco

Chapter 1 - Vernon

A loud, grumbling noise woke Vernon up from a deep sleep.

"What was that?" he said aloud to himself, rolling over in his coffin. The noise grumbled again, but this time Vernon felt it.

"It's my tummy... wow, I'm really hungry!"

He'd gone to his Aunt Fiona's house for dinner last night but hadn't eaten a thing.

Rubbing his tummy, Vernon got up to see his pet tarantula, Mikey.

"I bet you're hungry too, Mikey," Vernon said, giving Mikey some bugs.

"You'd have hated the food at Aunt Fiona's, there were blood burgers, strawberry blood shakes, peppered blood steaks… yuck, yuck, yuck!"

Vernon wrinkled his nose in disgust.

"Arrrrragh," sighed Vernon, stretching his arms in the air. "Best get ready for school."

He combed his hair, washed his face and brushed his fangs.

Downstairs in the kitchen sat Vernon's parents, eating their breakfast.

"Morning," said Vernon.

"Hello Son," said his dad, biting into a leg of lamb. The lamb was raw, with the wool and skin still on. Blood dripped down his dad's chin.

"Urgh, Dad, that's gross… and it stinks!" Vernon said, beginning to feel hot and sticky. "I'm going to be sick."

Vernon ran out of the kitchen, grabbing his school lunch. Once outside he did a loud burp.

"Arr, that's better, it's only a bit of blood," he told himself, shaking his head as he began walking to school.

At Vernon's school, all the children were blood-sucking vampires, who ate meat and drank blood.

No-one there knew Vernon hated the sight of blood.

No-one knew he hated the smell of meat.

No-one knew Vernon was a vegetarian vampire, because it was his biggest secret!

Chapter 2 - School

As soon as Vernon walked through the school's gates, he saw Big Brian the Bully.

"Oi, Blood Breath! What've you got in your lunch box? Cranberry juice?" Brian yelled at Vernon.

"Whatever," Vernon whispered, looking for his friends.

"Oi, Small Fangs! I'm talking to you!" yelled Brian. Brian was with some other children, who began laughing.

Vernon's hands started to shake.

"Vernon... come over here!" said a different

voice.

It was Malcolm, Vernon's best friend. He had a copy of *Vampire's Weekly* magazine in his hand.

Vernon quickly walked to him.

"Is Brian picking on you again?" Malcolm asked.

"Yeah… he's just a stupid vampire," Vernon said, as he tried to stop his hands shaking.

The whistle blew and everyone started to make their way to class.

"Hey Vernon, look at this picture of a 𝔇𝔢𝔞𝔡𝔩𝔶 𝔙𝔞𝔪𝔭𝔦𝔯𝔢," Malcolm said, showing Vernon the magazine.

"Yeah… they're really scary!" Vernon said. "My dad knew one once; he had pointy teeth, only drank blood and came out after dark."

"Wow, if your dad knew one, he's lucky to be alive," Malcolm said.

"**Deadly Vampires** can scare other vampires to death!"

Vernon shivered, "I never want to see a **Deadly Vampire**!"

"Are you going to the Halloween disco?" Malcolm asked.

"When is it?" Vernon said.

"Next month. There'll be a band called Screaming Vampires and blood burger vans."

"Oh... great," said Vernon sadly, there'd be nothing for him to eat.

"And..." continued Malcolm, "Veronica's going to be there!"

"Really?" smiled Vernon, "Veronica's the prettiest vampire I've ever seen."

They arrived at class and Vernon sat down at his desk waiting for Veronica to arrive.

Chapter 3 – Veronica

Veronica walked in, her black hair swinging around her tiny shoulders.

"Oi, Small Fangs! Why you staring at Veronica?"

Vernon looked up to see Big Brian looking down at him.

"Erm... I wasn't," Vernon said, his face turning pink.

"Yes you were! Don't ask her to the Halloween disco, Small Fangs, cos she's going with me!"

Veronica's head sprung up in surprise. She

wrinkled her nose at Brian.

Mr Coffins entered the classroom.

"Sit down everybody," he said.

Big Brian tutted and walked past Vernon's desk, pushing Vernon's book to the floor.

Vernon sighed, bending to get it but Veronica already had it. She smiled and gave it to him. Vernon's face went even pinker!

If only he could go to the Halloween disco with Veronica. She'd never go with a vegetarian vampire though, he thought.

Then Vernon had an idea! What if he became a scary Deadly Vampire?

Surely that would impress Veronica and teach Big Brian a lesson or two!

Chapter 4 - The Plan

After school Vernon walked home with Malcolm.

"How do you become a Deadly Vampire?" Vernon asked.

"Well, you would have to eat lots of meat," replied Malcolm, looking at his *Vampire's Weekly* magazine. "Then you'd have to scare someone."

"I couldn't scare anyone," said Vernon, shaking his head.

"And lastly, you'd have to turn into a bat!" Malcolm started flapping his arms and ran round in circles.

"You look nothing like a bat!" Vernon said laughing.

At home, Vernon put Mikey on his bed and started to think of a plan.

"Mikey, I couldn't eat a whole animal, I'd be sick!" Vernon said.

"I definitely couldn't eat a chicken, they're full of feathers." Vernon laughed, as he imagined chasing a chicken, round and round in circles. "Best to avoid birds with sharp beaks!" Mikey put a leg across his own nose.

"Maybe a slower animal... like a tortoise," Vernon thought carefully.

Mikey began crawling quickly across the bed.

"But they've got a hard shell and look chewy." Vernon sighed and picked Mikey up. Mikey's eyes grew bigger.

"Of course there's you Mikey... I could eat you!" Vernon laughed. Mikey tried to jump out of Vernon's hands.

"I'm joking! I'd never eat you!" said Vernon, stroking Mikey.

"I need a short-haired animal which is big and heavy, so I can grab it quickly."

Vernon thought long and hard.

Then he jumped off the bed.

"I've got it Mikey! I know what I'm going to eat; there's lots of them and no-one will notice one missing!"

Vernon smiled.

"I'm going to eat a cow!"

Chapter 5 - The Cow

Early the next day, Vernon walked to a field full of cows.

'Humm… I'll just bite one leg,' thought Vernon.

He chose a small cow by the gate and slowly crept up to it. Vernon looked at its leg; it was covered in mud.

"Urgh… gross!" Vernon whispered.

Vernon ran up to the cow and jumped on its bottom. Leaning downwards, he grabbed its leg and opened his mouth wide. Closing his eyes, Vernon took one last gulp of air and stuck his fangs into the cow.

"Mooooooo!" cried the cow and shook its leg. Vernon flew through the air and landed in the hedge.

"Ouch!" said Vernon, pulling himself out. He was covered in leaves and twigs.

"Sorry Cow," Vernon said, looking at its leg.

"My fangs haven't even made a scratch mark," said Vernon. "I'm hopeless at this."

"Mooooooo," said the cow.

Vernon looked at his watch, it was time for school. He'd have to try meat another time.

Whilst walking to school Vernon thought about the next stage of his plan.

He needed to scare someone, but how could he, Vernon, possibly scare anyone?

Chapter 6 - Deadly Soup

"What was that noise?" Malcolm asked.

Vernon rubbed his belly, "It's my tummy, I'm hungry." They were sat together in the school canteen.

"What have you got for lunch?" said Malcolm.

"Cold chicken blood soup," lied Vernon, it was actually tomato and garlic soup.

Only vegetarian vampires could eat garlic. It made normal blood-sucking vampires sick for days.

"I've got a raw pig's nose," said Malcolm.

"Yuck!" thought Vernon and he looked away, only to see Big Brian the Bully.

"Oi, Small Fangs... what've you got in your bottle?" Brian said, grabbing Vernon's flask of soup.

"Hey... give me that back!" said Vernon.

"Oooh, cold blood, don't you want to share it?" said Big Brian. He then threw his head back and began drinking the soup.

"NO STOP! IT WILL MAKE YOU SICK!" Vernon yelled, jumping up.

Brian drank all the soup and let out a massive burp. He started to laugh but stopped suddenly and touched his tummy. It was making a strange, gurgling noise.

Big Brian burped again, and again, and then he was on the floor rolling from side to side.

"Arrrrgh! My stomach... arrrrgh!" cried Big

Brian.

Mr Coffins ran over.

"Vernon's poisoned me!" Brian moaned, tears spilling down his face.

"There was garlic in my soup Sir," Vernon whispered to Mr Coffins.

Mr Coffins shook his head.

"Off to the medical room Brian," he said and carried Brian out of the canteen.

Vernon looked at Malcolm.

"Oh no... I think I've scared Big Brian to death," he said.

Chapter 7 ~ Bats

Big Brian was away from school for a whole week!

"Wow Vernon! You really scared Brian with your soup!" said Malcolm.

"I know, it's great!" said Vernon, pleased to have completed the second part of his plan. They were sat at their desks waiting for Mr Coffins.

"There's only one week until the Halloween Disco," said Malcolm.

"Are you dressing up?" asked Vernon, looking at Veronica.

"Yes, as a ghost," said Malcolm.

"I'm coming as myself, a 𝕯𝖊𝖆𝖉𝖑𝖞 𝖁𝖆𝖒𝖕𝖎𝖗𝖊 bat," Vernon lied. Veronica looked up and smiled at him.

"Wow... I didn't know you could change into a bat, Vernon!" Malcolm said.

Vernon wondered if he'd be able to fool anyone.

Then Big Brian walked into the classroom; he had returned to school.

Brian went to Vernon's table and knocked his books on the floor.

"Brian! You shouldn't do that... Vernon is a 𝕯𝖊𝖆𝖉𝖑𝖞 𝖁𝖆𝖒𝖕𝖎𝖗𝖊!" Malcolm shouted.

Vernon gulped.

Brian stared at Vernon for a couple of seconds and then dropped his head back, roaring with laughter.

"That's the funniest thing I've ever heard!" said Brian, "If you're a 𝔇𝔢𝔞𝔡𝔩𝔶 𝔙𝔞𝔪𝔭𝔦𝔯𝔢, why've you got such small fangs?"

Vernon looked at the classroom door, hoping Mr Coffins would arrive.

"Well, 𝔇𝔢𝔞𝔡𝔩𝔶 𝔙𝔞𝔪𝔭𝔦𝔯𝔢," said Brian, "I challenge you to turn into a bat at the Halloween Disco, in front of everyone!"

"He's coming as a bat!" Malcolm said.

"Shut up Malcolm," Vernon said to his friend.

"I shall look forward to seeing you there, Small Fangs!" said Big Brian, laughing.

Mr Coffins arrived and Big Brian went to his own chair.

That night, Vernon watched telly with his dad.

"Dad, how do 𝕯𝖊𝖆𝖉𝖑𝖞 𝖁𝖆𝖒𝖕𝖎𝖗𝖊𝖘 turn into bats?" Vernon asked.

"It's in their blood son," said dad. "They just close their eyes, think of a bat and BINGO… they become a bat!"

"Could someone learn to become a bat?" asked Vernon.

"No, but there's a good shop in town that does bat costumes," said dad, smiling.

The next day after school, Vernon popped into town and visited the costume shop. There were all types of outfits to dress up in - witches, fairies, clowns… and bats!

Vernon tried on a couple of bat outfits until he found one that fitted perfectly. It was completely black, covered his head and had wings.

"FANGTASTIC! This should impress

Veronica!" he said, twirling around in front of the shop's mirror. Surely Big Brian would leave him alone now?

Chapter 8 – Halloween Disco

"Come on Vernon, I'm ready to go!" said Malcolm, who was bouncing around Vernon's house dressed as a ghost.

Vernon was in his bat costume in his bedroom.

"What do you think Mikey? Do I look like a real bat?"

Mikey sighed and closed his tarantula eyes.

"Veronica will think I look great," said Vernon, joining Malcolm to walk to school. "Big Brian won't pick on me now!"

Their school looked amazing! Corridors were filled with spooky lights, giant pumpkins and cobwebs. Screaming Vampires were playing in the main hall and there were tables full of blood burgers and blood juice.

"Can you see Big Brian?" shouted Vernon, over the music.

"No, but there's another vampire bat, just like you," said Malcolm, pointing to the corner of the room.

Malcolm went for a blood burger whilst Vernon went to see the vampire bat. It was Veronica!

"Veronica, are you a 𝕯𝖊𝖆𝖉𝖑𝖞 𝖁𝖆𝖒𝖕𝖎𝖗𝖊?" Vernon asked.

"No it's just a really good costume, like yours!" she said.

Vernon's face went red. Veronica knew he

wasn't a 𝔇𝔢𝔞𝔡𝔩𝔶 𝔙𝔞𝔪𝔭𝔦𝔯𝔢.

He opened his mouth to explain when a loud voice shouted...

"Oi... Small Fangs! Let's see ya wings!"

It was Big Brian; he was in jeans and a t-shirt.

"Ha ha, Small Fangs thinks he's a 𝔇𝔢𝔞𝔡𝔩𝔶 𝔙𝔞𝔪𝔭𝔦𝔯𝔢!" said Big Brian.

"Go away Brian," said Vernon quietly.

Instead Big Brian walked up to Vernon and began pulling at his costume.

"Get off, Brian!" Vernon shouted, but it was too late. Vernon's costume ripped down his arm.

"Ha ha! It's just a costume! You'd never be a 𝔇𝔢𝔞𝔡𝔩𝔶 𝔙𝔞𝔪𝔭𝔦𝔯𝔢, Small Fangs!" Big Brian said.

Everyone in the school hall looked at Vernon. He looked at his ripped costume and felt angry, really angry.

Veronica took Vernon's arm and tried to pull him away.

"No Veronica, I'm fed up of Brian making me look stupid."

Vernon faced Big Brian.

"Brian, you're just a boring, normal blood-sucking vampire. You can't turn into a bat either!" he shouted.

"I could if I wanted to!" said Brian.

"Go on then!" Vernon said. All the other children stood around Big Brian waiting.

"Fine, Small Fangs, I will!" said Big Brian.

Big Brian closed his eyes, he held his breath and began making loud whining noises. He closed his hands together and began squeezing them hard; his face started to go red. Everyone waited, the hall was silent.

Big Brian's face got redder and redder until he turned purple. Suddenly he let out a big gasp of air and fell to the floor.

Vernon ran to Big Brian's side and shook his arm. Brian started to moan.

"Arrrrgh... what happened?" Brian cried.

"You fainted!" said Vernon.

The room exploded with laughter.

Mr Coffins arrived and helped Big Brian to his feet. "Come on Brian, let's go to the medical room... again," said Mr Coffins.

All the children went back to eating burgers and listening to the band.

Vernon smiled to himself. Big Brian wouldn't be bothering him for a while.

Then someone took hold of Vernon's hand. It was Veronica.

"So do you want a blood burger?" she asked.

"No… to be honest, I hate them." Vernon said, looking at his shoes.

"Me too, I'd much rather a veggie burger!" said Veronica.

"What?" Vernon's eyes grew larger.

"I'm a vegetarian vampire!" said Veronica. "My mum gave me some vegetable burgers in my school bag, do you want one?"

"I'd love one!" said Vernon smiling.

Both dressed up as the deadliest vampires of the night, Vernon and Veronica secretly sunk their fangs into vegetarian burgers!

When Vernon got home he got Mikey out to play.

"It's not so bad being a vegetarian vampire, after all!" said Vernon, and that night he fell asleep with a full tummy!

About the Author

Helen Wendy Cooper lives in Worcestershire, England, with her boyfriend, two cats, a tortoise, three turtles and four fish.

She thinks writing and drawing for children is fun, fun, fun!

Helen's had a few day jobs too, including being a military musician, a nursery nurse and working for the Police.

Helen started writing children's books for her GCSEs when she was 14 years old.

She hopes you enjoy her stories!

COMING SOON...

THE VEGETARIAN VAMPIRE:

THE LOST FANGS!